THE GIANT CARROT

JAN PECK   pictures by BARRY ROOT

Dial Books for Young Readers ❧ New York

With love to my father, mother, brother, and sister—J.P.
For Janna Margaret Marian—B.R.

Published by Dial Books for Young Readers
A member of Penguin Putnam Inc.
375 Hudson Street
New York, New York 10014

Text copyright © 1998 by Jan Peck
Pictures copyright © 1998 by Barrett V. Root
All rights reserved
Designed by Nancy R. Leo
Printed in Hong Kong
First Edition
5 7 9 10 8 6 4

Library of Congress Cataloging in Publication Data
Peck, Jan.
The giant carrot / Jan Peck; pictures by Barry Root.—1st ed.
p.   cm.
An adaptation of the Russian folktale "The turnip."
Summary: Little Isabelle surprises her family with her unique
way of helping a carrot seed grow and of getting the huge vegetable
from the ground. Includes a recipe for carrot pudding.
ISBN 0-8037-1823-3 (trade).—ISBN 0-8037-1824-1 (lib. bdg.)
[1. Carrots—Folklore. 2. Folklore—Russia.]
I. Root, Barry, ill. II. Turnip. III. Title.
PZ8.1.P33Gi 1998   398.2'0947'042—dc20   [E]   95-38069   CIP   AC

The artwork was prepared using watercolor and gouache on
Arches 140-lb. hot-press watercolor paper.

Author's Note

    I adapted *The Giant Carrot* from the Russian folktale "The Turnip." Folklorists call this story a "chain formula" tale because it is a series of linked characters. Russian minstrels may have first told "The Turnip" as early as the twelfth century. In the mid-1800's, Russian folklorist Alexander Afanasyev published it in one of his folklore anthologies.

    Alice Dalgliesh and Katherine Milhous collected the first American version from a Russian storyteller in their book *Once on a Time*, published in 1938. I have read and heard many variations of the tale, including Norbert Guterman's translation of Afanasyev's tale in his book *Russian Fairy Tales*, published in 1945. As a longtime gardener and cook, I chose to replace the turnip of the story with the tasty, versatile carrot.

One warm spring day tall Papa Joe said, "I will plant a carrot seed. And come summer, when it's grown, I'll drink a tall glass of carrot juice."

Smacking his lips, he grabbed his shovel. He dug in the sandy soil until it was as fine and fluffy as stone-ground flour.

Wide Mama Bess hollered from the kitchen door, "Whatcha doin', Papa Joe?"

"Plantin' a carrot seed, so come summer, I can drink a tall glass of carrot juice," said Papa Joe.

Wide Mama Bess sauntered over to him. "I'd rather park my lips on a wide bowl of carrot stew."

She leaned over and poked one fingertip into the soil. She reached into her apron pocket and pulled out a small box. Inside lay one teeny-tiny carrot seed. She dropped it into the hole, covered it with soil, and patted it down.

"There," she said.

Up walked strong Brother Abel. "Whatcha doin',
Mama Bess?"

"Plantin' a carrot seed, so come summer, I'll have a
wide bowl of carrot stew."

Brother Abel dipped a bucket into the well. He
carried water to where Mama Bess had planted the
seed. He scooped the water in his strong hands and
sprinkled it over the soil.

"I've got my mouth set on a jar of strong carrot relish,"
he said.

Mama Bess and Papa Joe shook their
heads.

"No," Papa Joe said, "I want a tall glass
of carrot juice."

"No," Mama Bess said, "I want a wide
bowl of carrot stew."

Just then the screen door swung open and out skipped sweet Little Isabelle. "Whatcha doin', Brother Abel?"

"Waterin' a carrot seed, so come summer, I'll have a jar of strong carrot relish."

Sweet Little Isabelle skipped over to where her family stood. "I want to help too," she said.

Brother Abel laughed. "What can you do?"

"I'll sing and dance to the carrot to make it grow. And come summer, we'll have little cups of sweet carrot puddin'."

Tall Papa Joe, wide Mama Bess, and strong Brother Abel laughed. But when sweet Little Isabelle sang and danced around the carrot seed, two tiny leaves sprang right up through the soil.

As the days grew brighter, Papa Joe raked leaves around the carrot top. Mama Bess pulled weeds, and Brother Abel sprinkled water. The carrot top grew a little bit.

But when sweet Little Isabelle sang and danced around the carrot top, it grew until it was as tall as Little Isabelle.

Papa Joe scratched his head. "Well, don't that beat all. That carrot sure takes a fancy to Little Isabelle's singin' and dancin'."

As the days grew warmer, Papa Joe tossed hay around the carrot top. Mama Bess pulled weeds, and Brother Abel sprinkled water. The carrot top grew a little bit.

But when sweet Little Isabelle sang and danced around the carrot top, it grew and grew until it was as tall as Mama Bess.

Mama Bess wiped her face with her apron. "Well, I do declare. That carrot sure cottons to Little Isabelle's singin' and dancin'."

As the days grew longer, Papa Joe shoveled compost around the carrot top. Mama Bess pulled weeds, and Brother Abel sprinkled water. The carrot top grew a little bit.

But when sweet Little Isabelle sang and danced around the carrot top, it grew and grew and grew until it was as tall as Brother Abel.

Brother Abel dusted off his overalls. "Well, for cryin' in a bucket. That carrot sure takes a shine to Little Isabelle's singin' and dancin'."

One summer day when sweet Little Isabelle sang and danced around the carrot top, her song fell like a gentle summer rain and her heels kicked up a soft summer breeze.

The carrot top grew and grew and grew until it was as tall as Papa Joe.

"Today I'm going to pick this carrot. I want a tall glass of carrot juice," Papa Joe said.

Mama Bess stuck out her chin. "*I'm* going to pick this carrot. I want a wide bowl of carrot stew."

Brother Abel shook his head. "*I'M* going to pick this carrot. I want a jar of strong carrot relish."

"Please, let me help," Little Isabelle
cried. "We'll have little cups of sweet
carrot puddin'."

But Papa Joe grabbed hold of the
carrot top first and yanked as hard
as he could. He huffed and
tugged and puffed and pulled.
The carrot didn't budge.

"Will you help me, Mama Bess?" Papa Joe finally asked.

"Of course I will." She wrapped her arms around Papa Joe's belly, and they huffed and tugged and puffed and pulled. The carrot didn't budge.

"You're strong, Brother Abel. Help us pull up this carrot," Mama Bess said.

Brother Abel popped his knuckles. "Sure thing."

Papa Joe grabbed the carrot top. Mama Bess wrapped her arms around his belly. Brother Abel hugged Mama Bess's middle. And they huffed and tugged and puffed and pulled.

The carrot didn't budge.

"Please, let me help!" Little Isabelle cried. Tall Papa Joe, wide Mama Bess, and strong Brother Abel laughed.

Papa Joe winked. "Well, let's see what Little Isabelle can do."

Papa Joe grabbed the carrot top. Mama Bess wrapped her arms around Papa Joe. Brother Abel hugged Mama Bess. And sweet Little Isabelle held on to Brother Abel as she sang and danced.

The carrot began to shiver and shake and quiver and quake. And when Little Isabelle sang a high note—"Aaaah!"—the carrot popped right out of the ground.

Their eyes grew wide and their mouths fell halfway to their toes. The carrot was as tall as tall Papa Joe, as wide as wide Mama Bess. And because it was so hard to pull out of the ground, they knew it was even stronger than strong Brother Abel.

And when at last they sat down at the table with their tall glasses of carrot juice, wide bowls of carrot stew, jars of strong carrot relish, and little cups of carrot puddin', they all agreed—the puddin' was as sweet as sweet Little Isabelle.

Little Isabelle's Carrot Puddin'

(Ask Mama or Papa to help you.)

Combine and blend until smooth:

- 1 cup peeled and grated carrots
- 1/2 cup milk
- 2 whole eggs
- 1/2 teaspoon nutmeg
- 1/2 teaspoon cinnamon
- 2 tablespoons melted butter
- 1 cup honey (I told you it's as sweet as Little Isabelle.)

When smooth, stir in gently:

- 4 slices bread, cut into cubes
- 1/4 cup raisins
- 1/4 cup chopped nuts

Pour into greased baking dish.
Bake for one hour at 350°F.
Serve hot or cold in coffee cups.
Delicious with ice cream too.